A Note to Parents and Caregivers:

Read-it! Readers are for children who are just starting on the amazing road to reading. These beautiful books support both the acquisition of reading skills and the love of books.

The PURPLE LEVEL presents basic topics and objects using high frequency words and simple language patterns.

The RED LEVEL presents familiar topics using common words and repeating sentence patterns.

The BLUE LEVEL presents new ideas using a larger vocabulary and varied sentence structure.

The YELLOW LEVEL presents more challenging ideas, a broad vocabulary, and wide variety in sentence structure.

The GREEN LEVEL presents more complex ideas, an extended vocabulary range, and expanded language structures.

The ORANGE LEVEL presents a wide range of ideas and concepts using challenging vocabulary and complex language structures.

When sharing a book with your child, read in short stretches, pausing often to talk about the pictures. Have your child turn the pages and point to the pictures and familiar words. And be sure to reread favorite stories or parts of stories.

There is no right or wrong way to share books with children. Find time to read with your child, and pass on the legacy of literacy.

Adria F. Klein, Ph.D.
Professor Emeritus
California State University
San Bernardino, California

Editor: Jacqueline A. Wolfe
Designer: Nathan Gassman
Page Production: Angela Kilmer
Creative Director: Keith Griffin
Editorial Director: Carol Jones
The illustrations in this book were created digitally.

Picture Window Books
5115 Excelsior Boulevard
Suite 232
Minneapolis, MN 55416
877-845-8392
www.picturewindowbooks.com

Printed in the United States of America.

Library of Congress Cataloging-in-Publication Data
Jones, Christianne C.
Robin's new glasses / by Christianne C. Jones ; illustrated by Ji Sun Lee.
p. cm. — (Read-it! readers)
Summary: Robin worries about how life will change when she gets her first pair of glasses.
ISBN 1-4048-1587-2 (hard cover)
[1. Eyeglasses—Fiction.] I. Lee, Ji Sun, ill. II. Title. III. Series.

PZ7.J6823Rnu 2005
[E]—dc22   2005023151

Robin's
New Glasses

by Christianne C. Jones
illustrated by Ji Sun Lee

Special thanks to our advisers for their expertise:

Adria F. Klein, Ph.D.
Professor Emeritus, California State University
San Bernardino, California

Susan Kesselring, M.A.
Literacy Educator
Rosemount–Apple Valley–Eagan (Minnesota) School District

PICTURE WINDOW BOOKS
Minneapolis, Minnesota

Robin woke up extra early on
Monday morning.

It was a special day. Robin was getting her first pair of glasses.

Robin was nervous. Would everything change once she got glasses?

At the eye doctor, Robin couldn't sit still.

It was taking forever!

Finally, the doctor called Robin's name.

Her glasses were ready.

Robin put on her new glasses.

Wow! Everything was clear!

Robin loved her glasses. They were red. It was her favorite color.

The glasses made her feel so cool!

She loved how they looked.
She loved how they felt.

Most of all, Robin loved how well she could see.

She could finally read all the letters on the board.

Robin could still do everything she did before. In fact, she could do it better now that she could see!

23

More *Read-it!* Readers

Bright pictures and fun stories help you practice your reading skills. Look for more books at your level.

At the Beach 1-4048-0651-2
Bears on Ice 1-4048-1577-5
The Bossy Rooster 1-4048-0051-4
Dust Bunnies 1-4048-1168-0
Flying with Oliver 1-4048-1583-X
Frog Pajama Party 1-4048-1170-2
Jack's Party 1-4048-0060-3
The Lifeguard 1-4048-1584-8
The Playground Snake 1-4048-0556-7
Recycled! 1-4048-0068-9
The Sassy Monkey 1-4048-0058-1
Tuckerbean 1-4048-1591-0
What's Bugging Pamela? 1-4048-1189-3

Looking for a specific title or level? A complete list of *Read-it!* Readers is available on our Web site:
www.picturewindowbooks.com